Follow
my Leader

FACING UP To Responsibility

Gianni Padoan   Illustrated by Emanuela Collini

FACING UP SERIES

Other titles

Break-up

Remembering Grandad

Danger Kid

© 1987 Happy Books Milan Italy
English language Edition © Child's Play (International) Ltd
This impression 1990

ISBN 0-85953-313-1
Printed in Singapore

It was great when Wayne first
moved in. He was much older than me,
but he didn't seem to mind talking
to me. He even let me listen
to his tapes while he told me
about all the amazing things
he had done before he moved
to our street. He always had lots
of money on him.

The trouble was, my Mum didn't
seem to like me spending time
with him. If she saw us together,
she always seemed to want me to do
something, like water the garden,
wash the car, mow the lawn . . .
"Not again, Joe," moaned Wayne.
"Why don't you ever say No?"

I used to go around all the time with
my friends James and Gwen, but being
in Wayne's gang was much more exciting.
We had some great adventures, like
sneaking into people's gardens without
them knowing. No-one wanted to get into
trouble, but no-one wanted to be left
out, either. If you said you didn't want
to do something, the others called you
chicken. It was just like a game of
Follow My Leader.

Mum started going on and on about
Wayne. "You're silly," she said.
"He only lets smaller children
into his gang because
he can make them do what he wants.
You spend all your time with him,
and none with Gwen and James.
Why don't you ask them round
tonight?"

I didn't tell Mum, but I wasn't getting
on very well with James and Gwen.
We argued all the time.
"You're stupid!" Gwen used to say.
"Wayne's using you. You do just what
he tells you!"
"Rubbish!" I replied. "You sound just
like Mum!"

One night our gang played on the
building site. We weren't supposed to,
but we waited until the workmen had
gone. "Follow my Leader!" ordered Wayne.
"On bikes! Let's see who is the best!"

He set off around the building site on
his bike. Everyone had to follow him,
trying to do what he did. If you
couldn't, you were out. Wayne was
brilliant! He could do the best ramps
and wheelies I'd ever seen. No-one else
was anywhere near as good, and we all
dropped out until only Wayne was left.
"The winner!" he yelled. "I'm the best!"

Wayne and I walked back to our street,
talking about how good he was at bike-
riding. I really wished that Gwen or
James could see me then. There I was,
talking like a friend to someone almost
grown-up.

We held gang meetings every week,
in the tool shed in Danny's garden.
One day, it was raining, and there
was nothing to do.
"I'm bored," said Wayne. "Who wants
a smoke?"
"Hey!" said Danny. "Not in here!
My Dad would kill me if he found out."
"Smoking might kill you first," I said.
"It's really bad for you."
"Scared, are you?" jeered Wayne.
"Look, everyone! Joe's scared!"
"No, I'm not!" I protested. "Why do
something that is bad for you?"
"Suppose I dared you?" sneered Wayne.
"What would your excuse be then?"
Everyone was watching me. Wayne held
out the packet. I took a cigarette
and lit it. It tasted awful, but I tried
to pretend I was used to it. Everyone else
ended up smoking, but they all looked
as sick as I felt!

I saw James and Gwen later on that day, and they said I smelled like a chimney.

"I suppose you think you're grown up now," said Gwen.

"I couldn't say No. Wayne dared me!"

"And suppose he dared you to jump off a cliff?"

"It's not the same!"

"Yes it is! You're always off with that stupid gang! And when you're not, you're boring us with stories about what you've done!"

"*You're* the boring ones!" I shouted. "You sound just like my Mum! I'm fed up with both of you!"

After that, I didn't want to see James and Gwen ever again. I thought of them as little kids, while Wayne and I were like grown-ups. Once, when I called round to see him, Wayne was cooking his own lunch.

"Want some?" he asked.

"Yes, please!" I answered. "It looks great. I didn't know you could cook!"

"I guess that some people grow up quicker than others," smiled Wayne. "Like you and me. How do you like your eggs?"

After lunch, Wayne and I went to the
park to meet the others. We sat around,
listening to Wayne. He told us that
once he'd drunk a whole bottle of whisky
by himself, and borrowed his Dad's car.
He'd solved a robbery for the police
and had been on television. He had lots
more stories besides. James and Gwen
would have sneered and said he was
making them up, but I knew better.

On the way back from the park, we came across a fat kid playing tennis against the wall. He wasn't very good, and we started jeering and laughing when he missed the ball.

"Follow my Leader!" shouted Wayne. "Watch out, Fatty!"

We started playing football with his tennis balls, and throwing them over the wall. It was funny at first, but then Jason threw a ball into the fat kid's face. His glasses broke, and he started crying.

"Time to go!" called Wayne,
and everybody ran off.
I felt sorry for the fat kid,
and I stayed behind to help him
find all the bits of his glasses.

But then, his big brother turned up. "You should be ashamed of yourself!" he said to me, clipping my ear. "Seven onto one! You'd better save up your pocket money to'pay for my brother's glasses. Or else!"

I walked away. Perhaps being in Wayne's gang had its drawbacks. What happened next made up my mind.

We met up later in town, and everyone
laughed when I told them about being
caught.
I suggested having a collection to
pay for the fat kid's glasses.
"I don't have any money," said Wayne.
"And I need some batteries for my stereo.
Who's going to borrow some for me?"
"You don't mean *steal* them?" I asked.
"It's only a game," said Wayne,
smiling. "Only a dare. You wouldn't
turn down a dare, would you?"
Everyone was looking at me. I felt my
face go red.
"Yes," I said. "This isn't a game.
And it isn't funny."
I turned and walked away.
"Forget about him," Wayne said to the
others. "Come on. Follow my Leader!"

I was lucky I chose that moment to walk away. I heard later what had happened. Kevin had the job of putting the batteries in his pocket, and he had dropped one on the floor. The manager had grabbed him, and had called the police and Kevin's parents. The police let Kevin off with a warning, but his parents grounded him for six months.

Wayne had been outside the shop, acting as look-out. I used to think he was just lucky, but now I realised that he made sure he wasn't the one to get caught.

I didn't spend much time with the gang after that. Wayne and the others always seemed to be bullying smaller kids or teasing animals. Once, I caught them tying my cat's legs together.

I hadn't seen much of James or Gwen since our quarrel. I didn't want to admit that they had been right all along, so I pretended to them that I was still in the gang, and that I was still friends with Wayne. The only one to benefit from all this was my dog, Rufus. His paws must have been sore from all the walking we did!

One day, in the park, I saw Gwen and her friend Sarah writing in their diaries. Then I saw Wayne stop and make fun of them. Suddenly, he snatched Gwen's diary, and started to read it.
"Give it back!" yelled Gwen, but Wayne lifted the book out of her reach.

Without thinking, I ran up.
"Go on!" I yelled. "Give it back! Now!"
Wayne turned with a sneer.
"Oh, yes?" he said. "And who's going to
make me?"
"Me!" I shouted, reaching for the book.
Wayne put up a fist.
"And whose army?" he jeered.
I brought up my fists.
"Go on then!" said Gwen. "Beat up
someone half your size! It's all you're good
for! That, and getting other kids
to do your dirty work! Follow my Leader!
You never led anyone! You just pushed
them from the back!"
Wayne's eyes narrowed. He took a step
towards me. I waited for the punch, and
wondered what it was like to be knocked
out.

But then, after what seemed
like months, he stepped back.
He lowered his fist, and threw
the diary on the ground.
"Forget it," he said. "You're not
worth it. I don't want to read
the stupid book anyway."
He turned, and walked away down
the path. He looked smaller on his own,
without a gang around him.

My knees were trembling so much
I wanted to sit down, but I stood
and watched him walk away.
"Well done," said Sarah.
"Thanks," said Gwen. "At last
you've come to your senses.
Listen – Sarah and I
are meeting James later.
We are going to a barbecue.
Want to come? Or have you got
a gang meeting?"
I smiled. "I'll come with you," I said.
"I don't think I'll be playing
Follow my Leader any more!"